THE
TUNNEL

Written by
**Sarah
Howden**

Illustrated by
**Erika
Rodriguez
Medina**

Owlkids Books

SOMETHING BAD
happened. I don't like to
think about it.

Now it's just me and my
mom in the quiet house.

Mostly I sit in my room
and look out the window.
Sometimes Mom comes in
and hugs me tight.

I don't always hug her back.

People come to visit, and everyone has questions.

Tonight, it's Aunt Cheryl. She'll stare at me with her big eyes and ask, "Are you okay?"

I don't feel like talking.

So I find my plastic shovel,
choose a spot, and start to dig.

Down,

down

into the ground.

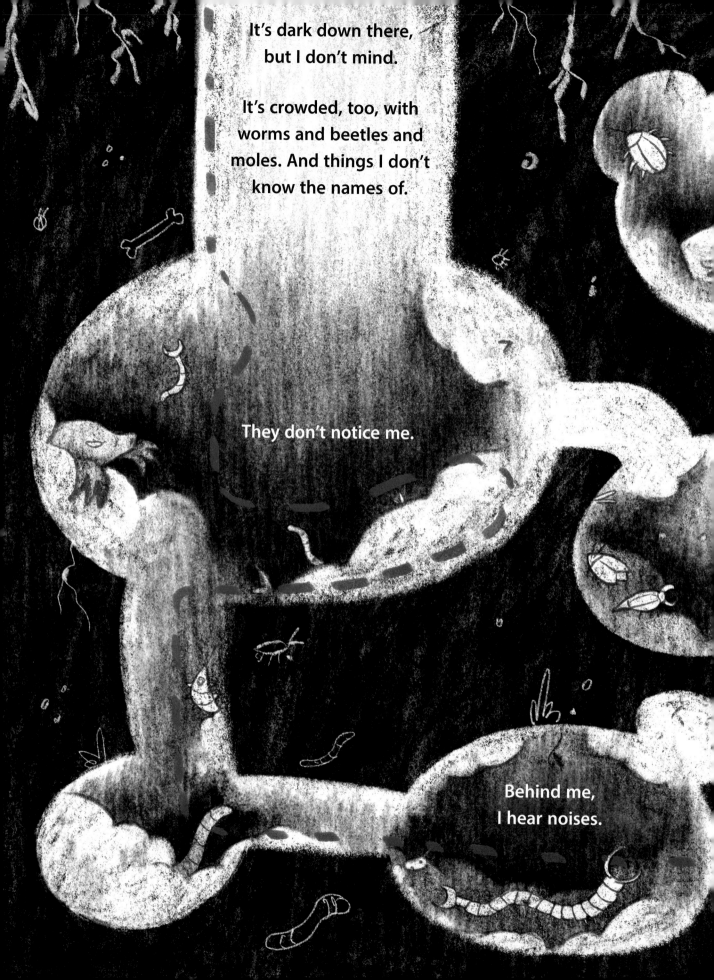

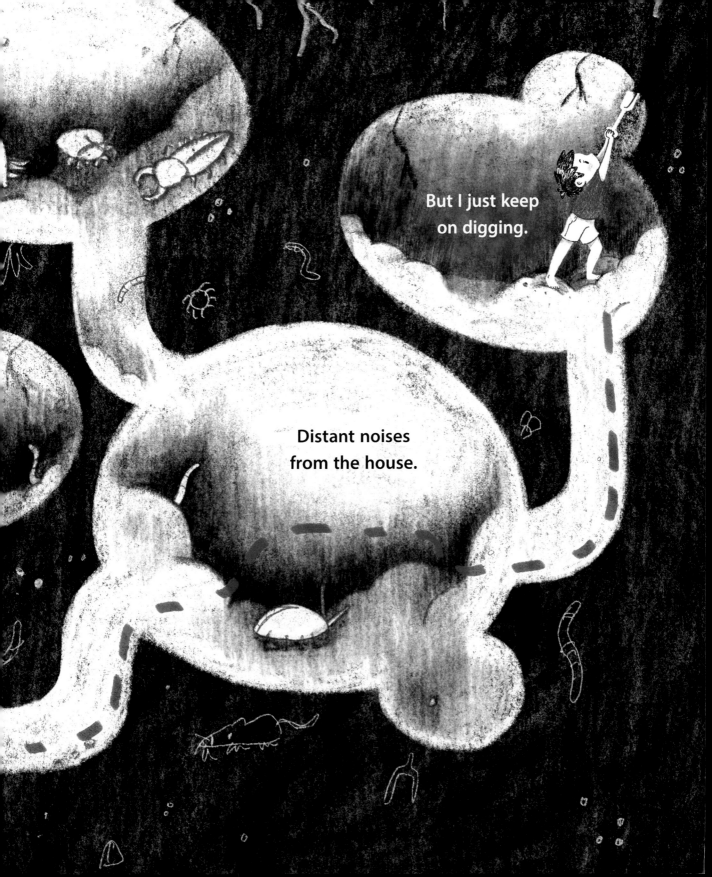

Then suddenly, I surface. I turn around, and there I am. Right in our backyard.

Through the windows, I see Mom and Aunt Cheryl.

I see the nightlight glowing in my room.

And then there's
the moon, between
the telephone wires.
A spotlight, clear
and certain.

"No one knows I'm out here,"
I tell the moon.

"I could just disappear."

I turn back to the window. Inside, Mom and
Aunt Cheryl are talking.

I watch them like they're on TV.

Mom turns in my direction. She can't see me,
but her face looks close enough to touch.

Almost like the moon.

And something shifts
inside me.

It nudges me like a
dog's nose.

I turn around and start to crawl.
Back the way I came.

This time, the worms know me.
The beetles, too.

The moles don't care either way.
They have their own
work to do.

The soil smells sweet and dark.
It smells like plants and rotten vegetables.

It smells like mud pies and old leaves and basements.

I'll go home for now,
I tell myself.
But I can always
come back.

The soil turns to carpet, and I tumble forward.

My room seems strange and square after
the tunnel. But I like it.

It's dim and cozy, and it's mine.

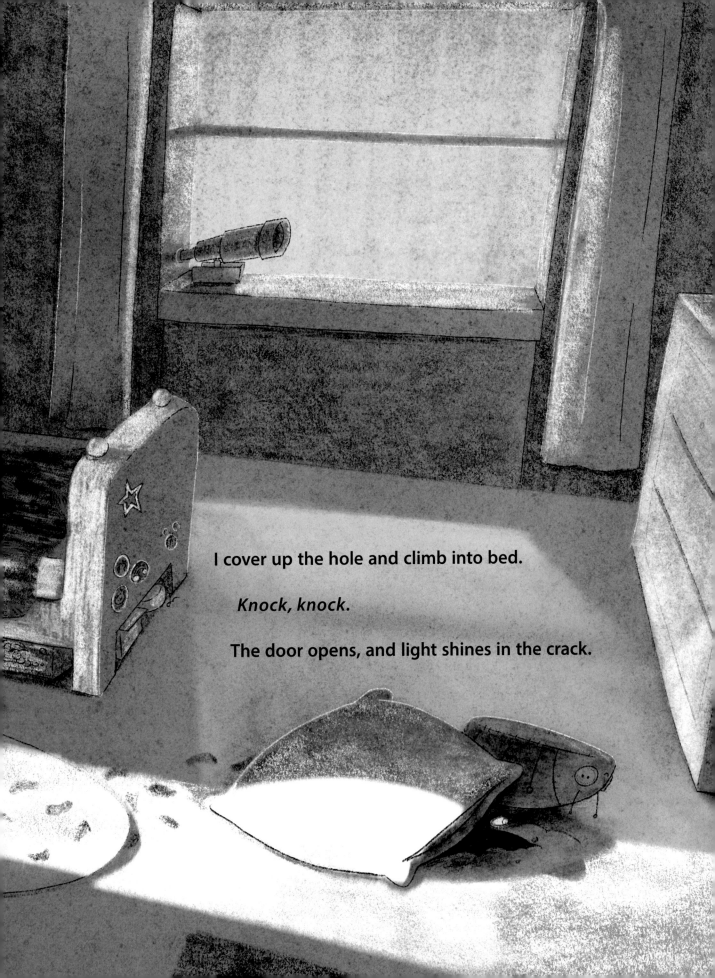

I cover up the hole and climb into bed.

Knock, knock.

The door opens, and light shines in the crack.

"May I come in?" Mom asks.

"Yes," I say. She sits down and gives me a hug. It's gentle and warm and strong.

Tonight, I hug her back.

As hard as I can.

Harder.

"What's this?" she asks, picking
something from my hair.

She holds it out—a crooked little twig.

I take it in my fingers. It feels like a bone.

"I made a tunnel out of here," I say.
"And then I came back."

Mom just nods.

I think she knows I need a secret place.
She might have secret places of her own.

I think she knows we sometimes travel far
away. Alone, where we don't have to talk.

"You came back,"
she says, and her face
is glowing in the soft light.

Just like the moon.

For A. —S.H.

*To all of those people in my life
who take care of me, but especially
to Lalo and to my dad* —E.R.M.

Owlkids Books acknowledges the financial support of the Canada Council for the Arts, the Ontario Arts Council, the Government of Canada through the Canada Book Fund (CBF) and the Government of Ontario through the Ontario Creates Book Initiative for our publishing activities.

Published in Canada by Owlkids Books Inc., 1 Eglinton Avenue East, Toronto, ON M4P 3A1
Published in the US by Owlkids Books Inc., 1700 Fourth Street, Berkeley, CA 94710

Library of Congress Control Number: 2021939050

Library and Archives Canada Cataloguing in Publication

Title: The tunnel / written by Sarah Howden ; illustrated by Erika Rodriguez Medina.
Names: Howden, Sarah, author. | Rodriguez Medina, Erika, illustrator.
Identifiers: Canadiana 20210212942 | ISBN 9781771474276 (hardcover)
Classification: LCC PS8615.O935 T86 2022 | DDC jC813/.6—dc23

Edited by Karen Li and Ella Russell | Designed by Alisa Baldwin

Manufactured in Shenzhen, Guangdong, China, in September 2021, by WKT Co.
Job #21B1031

A   B   C   D   E   F